APR 2 8 2005

Withdrawn/ABCL

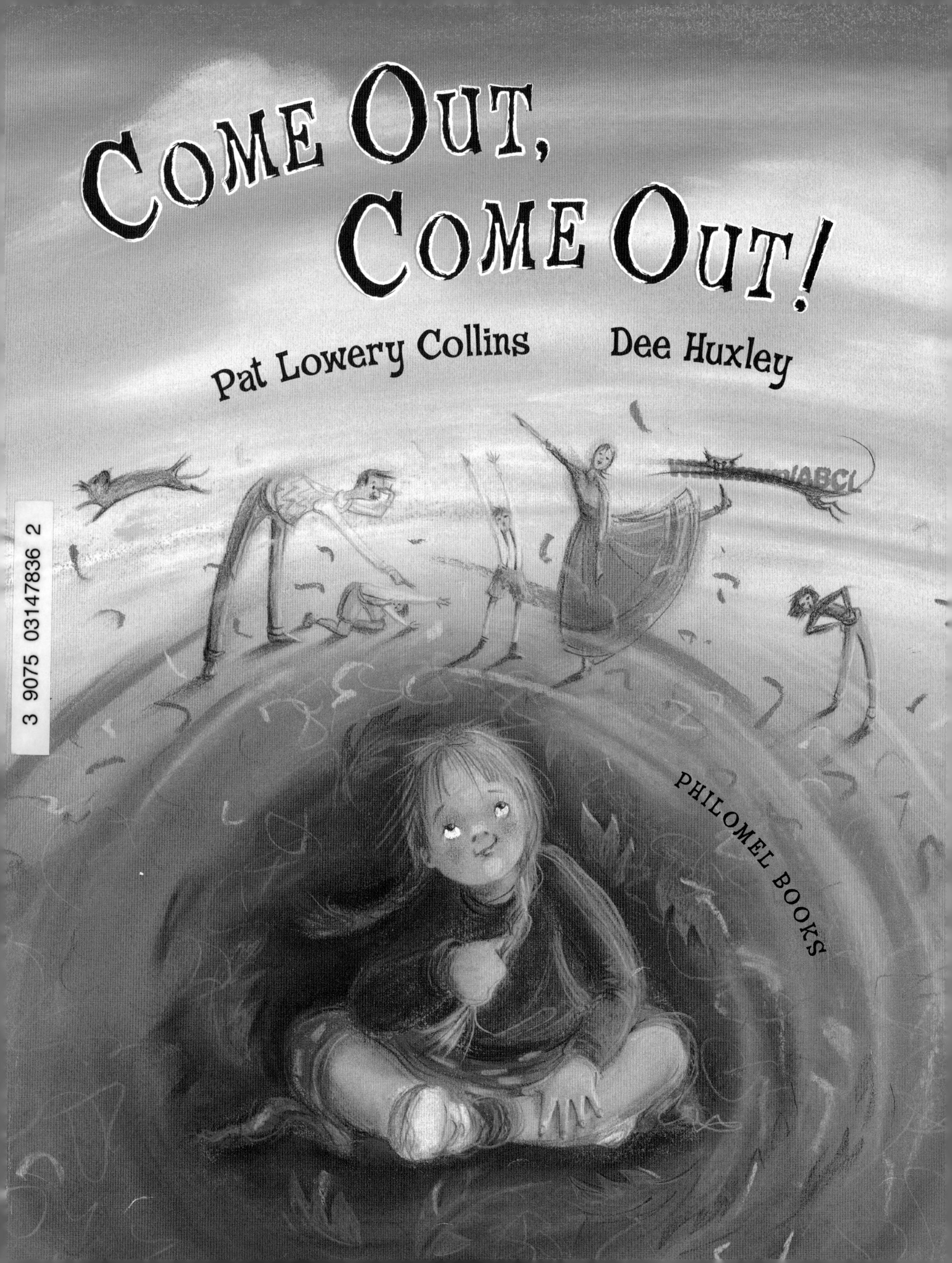
Come Out,
Come Out!
Pat Lowery Collins
Dee Huxley
PHILOMEL BOOKS

Hildy is hiding again.
"Where are you, Hildy?"
call the children.

“Where can Hildy be?”
asks her mother.
“Where in the world is Hildy?”
asks her father.

This time she will not answer.
"She is hiding again,"
say the children.
"She is hiding again,"
says her mother.
"I think we should look for her,"
says her father.

This time they will never find her.

"We've looked in a bird's nest," say the children.

"And in Mommy's button box."

"I've looked in a rabbit hole," says her mother.

"And up in the clouds."

"What a good idea, to look in the clouds," says her father.

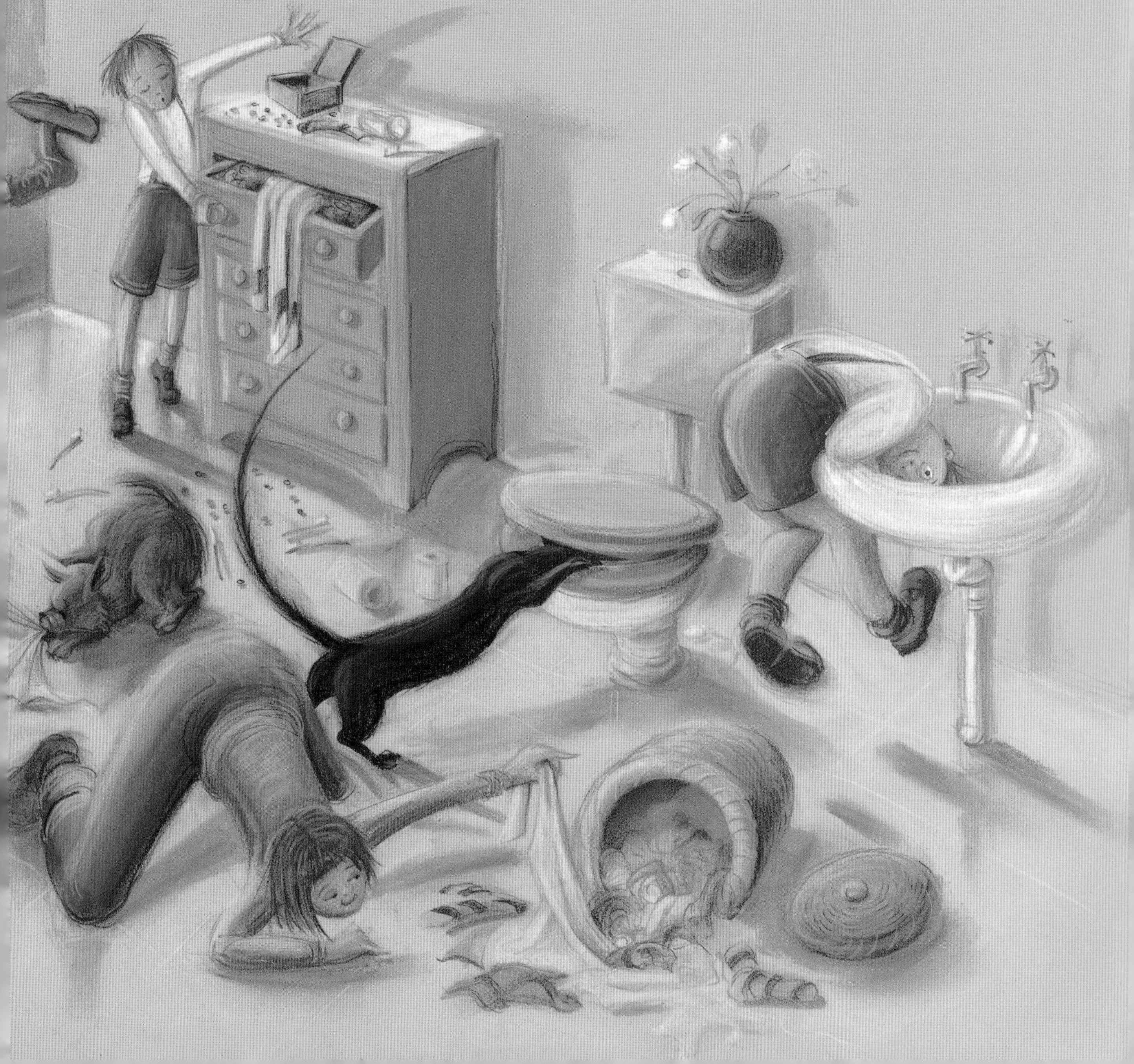

This time Hildy is so angry,
she will hide forever.
"She isn't up the chimney,"
say the children.
"She isn't sleeping inside the clock,"
says her mother.
"Hmmm. She isn't curled into my book,"
says her father.

This time she will never come out.
"Come out, come out,
wherever you are,"
call the children.
"Please come out, Hildy,"
says her mother.
"Please come out now,"
says her father.

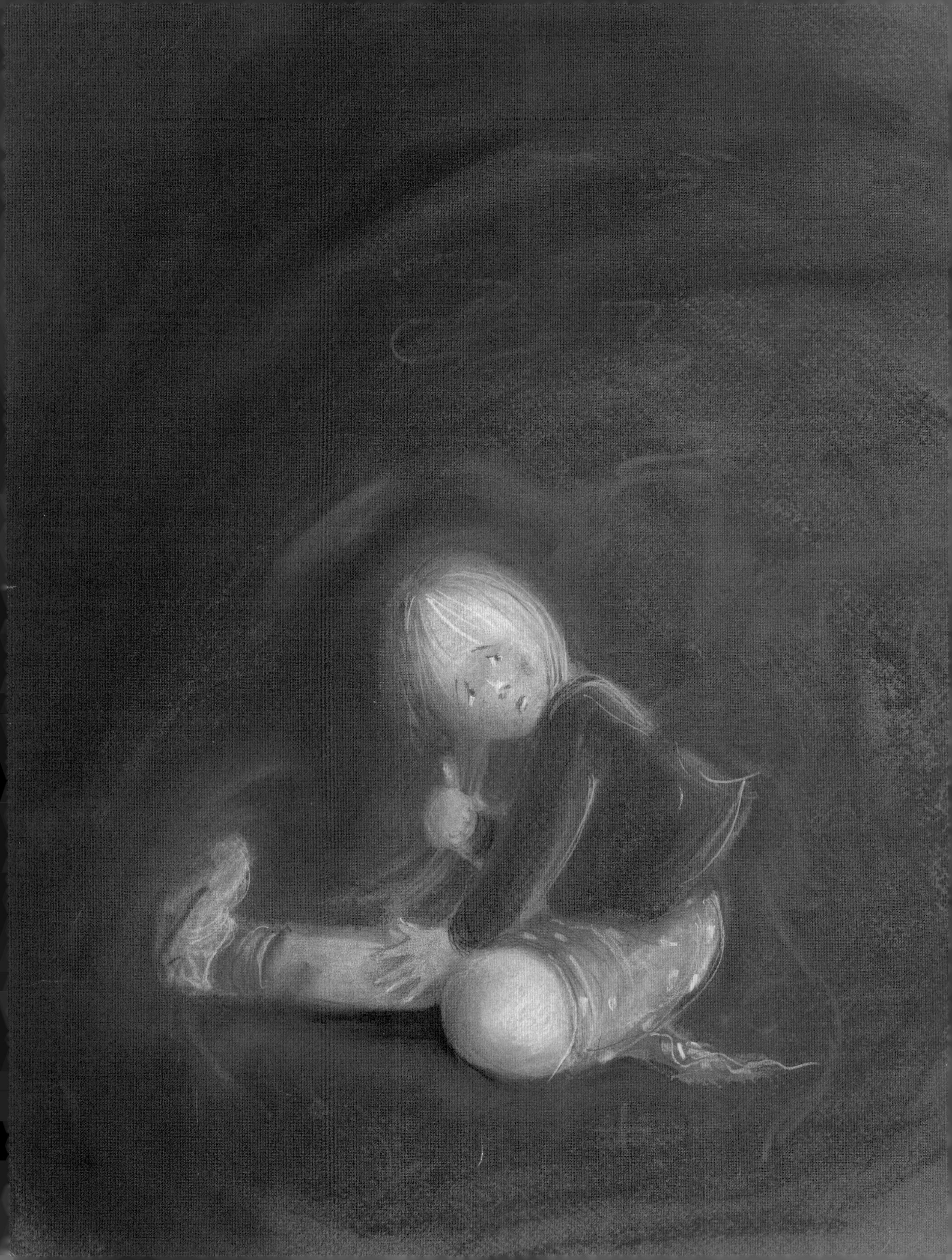

This time they are going to be
very,
very
sorry.
"We're sorry we didn't let you play,"
say the children.
"I'm sorry I was too busy to listen,"
says her mother.
"I'm sorry I didn't have time to fix your bike,"
says her father.

This time she will live with the birds and the animals.

"Come home, Hildy, before it gets dark," call the children.

"Come home, Hildy, before it gets cold," calls her mother.

"Come home, Hildy, before the cat eats your dinner," calls her father.

This time she will not be
tempted by anything.
"If you come out, Hildy,
you can name the new puppy,"
call the children.
"If you come out, Hildy,
you can move to a bigger bed,"
calls her mother.
"If you come out, Hildy,
you can have the last piece
of chocolate cake,"
says her father.

This time she will not make a sound.
"We think we heard her sneeze,"
say the children.
"I'm certain I heard her whisper,"
says her mother.
"Was that wind in the trees or Hildy singing?"
asks her father.

This time they are very close by.
"Did you hear that?"
ask the children.
"I'm sure I heard something,"
says her mother.
"I heard it, too,"
says her father.

This time she will
shut her eyes and lie
very,
very
still.
"Over there,"
say the children.
"In those leaves?"
asks her mother.
"It can't be little Hildy in all those leaves!"
says her father.

This time she will not cry.
"She was always our favorite,"
say the children.
"She was never cross with spiders,"
says her mother.
"She was so good to flies and bumblebees,"
says her father.

This time maybe THEY will cry.

"Someone has cast a spell over her," say the children.

"What can we do to wake her up?" asks her mother.

"Let me think," says her father.

This time she will not open
her eyes no matter what.
"Let's try tickles,"
say the children.
"Let's try kisses,"
says her mother.
"Let's try tickles
and kisses and hugs,"
says her father.
And they do.

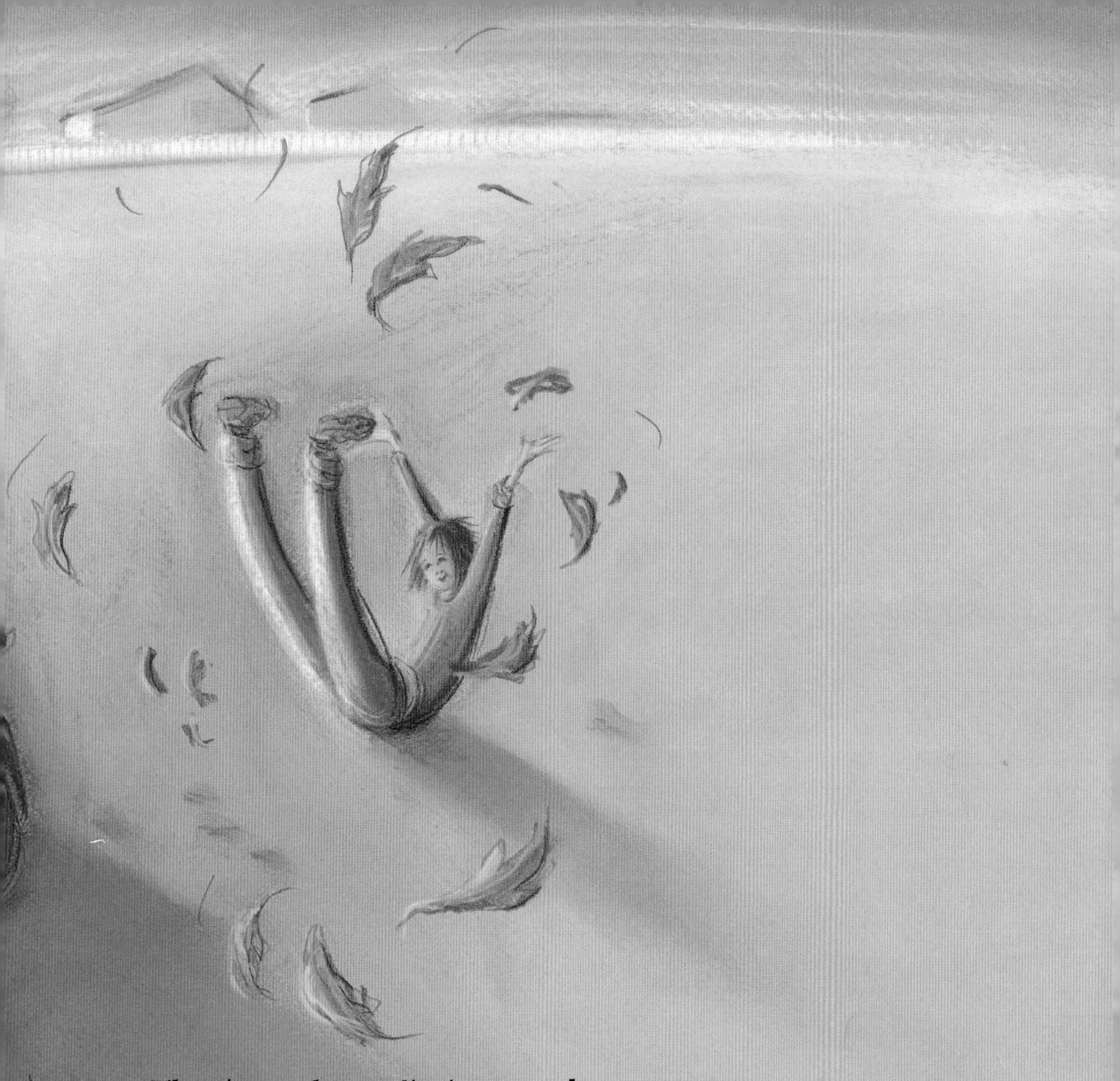

This time she can't stop giggling.

"We broke the spell!" say the children.

"We missed you so much," says her mother.

"We love you to pieces," says her father.

This time everything turned out just right.

To Timothy

–P. L. C.

Text copyright © 2005 by Pat Lowery Collins. Illustrations copyright © 2005 by Dee Huxley. All rights reserved. This book, or parts thereof, may not be reproduced in any form without permission in writing from the publisher, Philomel Books, a division of Penguin Young Readers Group, 345 Hudson Street, New York, NY 10014. Philomel Books, Reg. U.S. Pat. & Tm. Off. The scanning, uploading and distribution of this book via the Internet or via any other means without the permission of the publisher is illegal and punishable by law. Please purchase only authorized electronic editions, and do not participate in or encourage electronic piracy of copyrighted materials. Your support of the author's rights is appreciated. Published simultaneously in Canada. Manufactured in China by South China Printing Co. Ltd. Design by Gina DiMassi. The text is set in Fink Roman. The art was created with chalk pastels and colored pencils on Canson colored stock. Library of Congress Cataloging-in-Publication Data Collins, Pat Lowery. Come out, come out! / Pat Lowery Collins ; illustrated by Dee Huxley. p. cm. Summary: Hildy is so angry that she thinks she will hide from her family forever, but they manage to find her and make things right. [1. Behavior—Fiction. 2. Family life—Fiction. 3. Anger—Fiction.] I. Huxley, Dee, ill. II. Title. PZ7.C68353 Co 2005 [E]—dc21 2003008557 ISBN 0-399-23977-4

1 3 5 7 9 10 8 6 4 2

First Impression